little Miss Tidy

by Roger Hargreaves

WORLD INTERNATIONAL

Little Miss Tidy was an extraordinarily tidy person.

In Little Miss Tidy's house everything had its place.

She had a huge handbag.

Which she would fill with all sorts of things
until she had time to put them away tidily.

Then there were all her boxes.

She had small ones,
medium-sized ones,
big ones,
enormous ones,
round ones,
and square ones.

And this was where Little Miss Tidy
tidied away all her things.

Nothing was ever left lying around in her house.

Now, with all this tidying up going on
you would think that Little Miss Tidy
was perfect, wouldn't you?

Well she isn't!

On Monday, at nine o'clock,
she telephoned Mr Clever.

"As you are so clever," she said,
"could you tell me where I put my
hairbrush when I tidied up?"

On Tuesday, at ten o'clock,
she telephoned Mr Mean.

"As you like money so much," she said,
"could you tell me where I put my
purse when I tidied up?"

On Wednesday, at eleven o'clock,
she telephoned Mr Strong.

"As you like eggs so much," she said,
"could you tell me where I put my boiled
egg when I tidied up?"

On Thursday, at twelve o'clock,
she telephoned Mr Nosey.

"As you are always poking your nose into things,"
she said, "could you tell me where I put my
serving-spoon when I tidied up?"

On Friday, she didn't telephone anybody
because she had tidied away her telephone
and she had to run all the way to
Little Miss Chatterbox's house.

"As you love using the telephone," she said,
"could you tell me where I put my telephone
when I tidied up?"

Luckily, thanks to her friends, Little Miss Tidy
was able to find all the things she had
lost that week.

Her hairbrush was in a glove-box.

Her purse was in a shoe-box.

Her boiled egg was in the salt pot.

Her serving-spoon was in the tool-box.

And her telephone was in her sewing-box.

Little Miss Tidy certainly was very absent minded
when it came to remembering where she
had put things when she was tidying up.

But she couldn't help it.

On Saturday, it was her birthday and
Little Miss Chatterbox came to her house,
carrying a splendid-looking parcel all tied
up with red ribbon.

Little Miss Tidy couldn't wait to see what
was inside the present.

It was a notebook and pencil.

The perfect present for somebody who lost things as easily as Little Miss Tidy.

Little Miss Tidy was as happy as ...
well, as happy as Mr Happy.

She spent the rest of the day opening all her
boxes and writing down in her notebook
everything that she had stored away in them.

It was very late by the time she finished
her list.

She went to bed, very tired.

On Sunday morning, she woke with a start.

"My notebook and pencil!" she cried.

"Where ever did I put them when I tidied up?"

Little Miss Tidy spent all day Sunday
looking for her notebook and pencil.

She had to open and close all her boxes again.

And do you know where she eventually found her
notebook and pencil?

... on her bedside table!

SPECIAL OFFERS FOR MR MEN AND LITTLE MISS READERS

In every Mr Men and Little Miss book you will find a special token.
Collect only six tokens and we will send you a super poster of your choice
featuring all your favourite Mr Men or Little Miss friends.

And for the first 4,000 readers we hear from, we will send you a
Mr Men activity pad* and a bookmark* as well – absolutely free!

Return this page with six tokens from Mr Men and/or Little Miss books to:
Marketing Department, World International Limited, Deanway Technology Centre,
Wilmslow Road, Handforth, Cheshire SK9 3ET.

Your name:_____

Address:_____

_____

_____ Postcode: _____

Signature of parent or guardian: _____

I enclose **six** tokens – please send me a Mr Men poster ☐
I enclose **six** tokens – please send me a Little Miss poster ☐

We may occasionally wish to advise you of other children's books that
we publish. If you would rather we didn't, please tick this box ☐

*while stocks last   (Please note: this offer is limited to a maximum of two posters per household.)

Collect six of these tokens.
You will find one inside every
Mr Men and Little Miss book
which has this special offer.

1 TOKEN

Join the

MR. MEN & little miss Club

Treat your child to membership of the long-awaited Mr Men & Little Miss Club and see their delight when they receive a personal letter from Mr Happy and Little Miss Giggles, a club badge **with their name on**, and a superb Welcome Pack. And imagine how thrilled they'll be to receive a card from the Mr Men and Little Misses on their birthday and at Christmas!

Take a look at all of the great things in the Welcome Pack, every one of them of superb quality (*see box right*). If it were

on sale in the shops, the Pack alone would cost around £12.00. But a year's membership, including all of the other Club benefits, costs just **£7.99** (plus 70p postage) with a 14 day money-back guarantee if you're not delighted.

To enrol your child please send **your** name, address and telephone number together with **your child's** full name, date of birth and address (including postcode) and a cheque or postal order for £8.69 (payable to Mr Men & Little Miss Club) to: Mr Happy, Happyland (Dept. WI), PO Box 142, Horsham RH13 5FJ. Or call 01403 242727 to pay by credit card.

The Welcome Pack:

- ✓ Membership card
- ✓ Personalized badge
- ✓ Club members' cassette with Mr Men stories and songs
- ✓ Copy of Mr Men magazine
- ✓ Mr Men sticker book
- ✓ Tiny Mr Men flock figure
- ✓ Personal Mr Men notebook
- ✓ Mr Men bendy pen
- ✓ Mr Men eraser
- ✓ Mr Men book mark
- ✓ Mr Men key ring

Plus:

- ✓ Birthday card
- ✓ Christmas card
- ✓ Exclusive offers
- ✓ Easy way to order Mr Men & Little Miss merchandise

All for just £7·99! (plus 70p postage)

Please note: We reserve the right to change the terms of this offer (including the contents of the Welcome Pack) at any time but we offer a 14 day no-quibble money-back guarantee. We do not sell directly to children - all communications (except the Welcome Pack) will be via parents/guardians. After 31/12/96 please call to check that the price is still valid. Please allow 28 days for delivery. Promoter: Robell Media Promotions Limited, registered in England number 2852153.